BROTHERS GRIMM
The Most Beloved Fairy Tales

WSKids
WHITE STAR KIDS

ILLUSTRATIONS BY

MANUELA ADREANI

CONTENTS

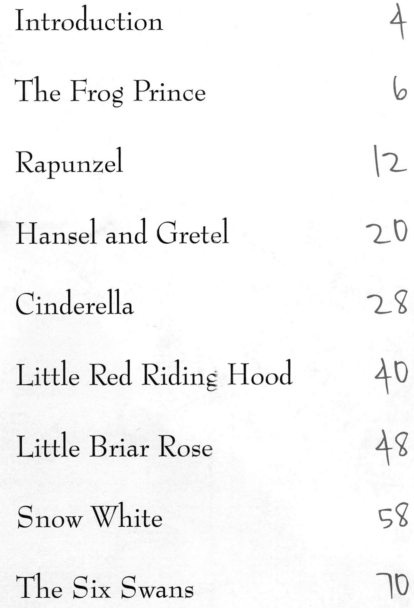

INTRODUCTION

There was a time when fairy tales only existed in the memory of those who told them. They were fantastical stories, set in magical and mysterious worlds in which courageous characters faced evil creatures, captivating the many children who listened to them before going to bed at night. People told these stories for a very long time, passing them down from generation to generation.

In the 19th century, two brothers called Jacob and Wilhelm Grimm became so passionate about these stories that they decided to do something that no one had ever done before: they traveled around their country listening to the most popular fairy tales, then wrote them down and put them all into a book, so that they would never be forgotten. It is therefore thanks to the Grimm brothers that these stories are still known and loved by children all over the world.

Fairy tales are able to travel in time and touch the hearts of children of all ages. They are great friends, offering us advice and giving us courage: when reading about Little Red Riding Hood and the wolf, we learn that we can never be too prudent, and the happy ending of the story of the Frog Prince teaches us that an act of kindness towards others will always make us happy. The daring fairy tale of the Six Swans teaches us that our love for our family makes it possible to face adversity with courage and even how to make shirts out of aster flowers.

So, never stop reading fairy tales and never stop telling them!

THE FROG PRINCE

Long ago in a faraway land there was a king who lived in a wealthy castle with his beloved daughters.

The daughters were all beautiful, but the youngest was so lovely that even the sun was dazzled whenever it caressed her face!

The castle was surrounded by a leafy garden, at the center of which was a pond. During the hottest hours of the day, the princess would seek shelter under the trees, where she often played with a golden ball. One day, with a throw that was stronger than usual, the precious ball landed into the water and sank to the bottom of the pond. The princess was furious for having lost her favorite pastime and cried desperately. But then, just as she resigned herself to wading through the pond to retrieve her ball, she heard a hoarse voice: "I can help you, if you wish!" The princess turned in the direction of the voice and to her surprise saw a frog sitting on a water lily.

"Here is your ball: I will return it to you if you make me a promise." Eager to get the ball back and without even thinking it over, the princess blurted out: "I'll give you anything: jewelry, gemstones, gold and silver!" The frog sat quietly then said: "I don't want any of those things. Promise me that you'll take me to the palace with you. I get very lonely here all on my own! I want to be in the palace and sit with you at the table, dance with you, play with you, and sleep in your bed. If you promise to care for me, to be my friend and to always stay with me, I will give you your ball."

The princess thought that she would never share her bed with a frog but she promised the frog everything he asked, just to get back her ball. As soon as he returned it, the princess laughed and ran back to the palace, quickly forgetting the incident.

A few hours later, during dinner, there was a strange sound: hop, hop, hop... It was the frog climbing the great staircase, he jumped one step at a time until he reached the king's table. The princess laughed and told her father what happened in the garden that morning, she remembered the silly promise she made to quickly and easily get her golden ball back. The king listened quietly then turned to his beloved daughter with a stern expression on his face and said: "Promises must always be kept; just because you are a princess doesn't excuse you from your commitments." Thus the girl was bound to keep her word.

The frog requested to be placed on the table and allowed to eat from the princess' gold plate. The girl agreed but was unable to touch any of her food. The prospect of having to spend the entire evening with this unwanted guest filled her with dread. What could a beautiful princess ever have in common with a revolting frog?

To her great surprise, the frog turned out to be very charming: he told her amusing stories that made her burst into laughter, and he listened to her secret thoughts and dreams without judgment; thus, the princess had a wonderful evening. When it was time to go to sleep, the frog reminded the princess of the promise that he could sleep next to her in her bed, under pure linen sheets embroidered with gold. The princess was horrified: how could she sleep next to a slimy frog?

And when the frog requested a goodnight kiss, the princess became so exasperated that she rudely replied: "Oh, no! I am never going to kiss you; my lips will never get close to your disgusting mouth!"

The frog was so hurt by those cruel words that his yellow eyes filled with tears. With two leaps he jumped onto the windowsill determined to leap back to the pond and forever leave behind the one who had so deeply humiliated him.

Only then did the princess realize just how cruel and superficial she had been: after all, had she not enjoyed the frog's company all evening?

Had they not laughed and joked like old friends?

And had she not confided in him unlike anyone before, revealing her innermost fears, insecurities and worries?

And had he not been the most understanding and sensitive of all people she had known until then?

To her great surprise she realized that she was thinking of the little frog as if he were a person, a sincere and trusted friend that she had now hurt.

Glowing with shame, she gave a long sigh and approached the frog. "Wait!" she said, "That was really rude of me. I acted foolishly and without thinking. I don't understand why you would care so much about someone like me, but if you still want a kiss, do come closer."

The frog turned to look at her with his calm and kind eyes and for a moment, the princess thought she could see him smiling.

Gently, she took him in her hands and pressed her lips against the frog's cold skin without feeling disgust or embarrassment.

A light wind tangled her long and beautiful hair, while a sweet distant melody began playing all around.

The princess felt enveloped by a strange feeling that was calm and reassuring: slowly she opened her eyes and looked at her little friend, but what she saw left her without words.

The frog was floating before her, in a whirlwind of golden sparks gleaming with magic light!

When all this ceased, instead of the frog there was a charming prince!

The girl was bewildered, hesitant and a little fearful, but the young man's gaze was loving and reassuring. He tenderly took her hand in his and began telling her his sad story. A long time ago, an evil and jealous witch had cast a spell on him, condemning him to live under the guise of a frog until he was kissed by a girl. At last, thanks to her, the spell had been broken and the prince was free to return to his home. As in all the best fairy tales, he asked the princess if she would take him as her husband and, with another kiss, she gave him her answer.

RAPUNZEL

In a small village surrounded by fields, there lived a man called Nicolas and his young wife, Anna. For many years they had dreamt of having a baby, but with no luck. Then one day their wish was finally granted. One beautiful spring day she sat at the window, longing to go outside. "I wish I had a garden like that," she said, looking at their neighbor's garden, which was full of all sorts of wonderful flowers and plants. "I would cook those delicious-looking vegetables!"

Their elderly neighbor spent all her time tending to her garden. In the village it was rumored that she was a witch, who used spells and potions to grow magical plants – and indeed, a witch she was. Anna thought the rapunzel looked especially delicious. So when Nicolas came home she said, "You wanted to give me a surprise for dinner. Well, I would like some rapunzel, please!"

"Where will I find that?" said Nicolas.

"There, in our neighbor's garden," she said, pointing.

"You want me to sneak into the garden of that witch? What if she catches me?" Nicolas replied.

"Well, don't get caught!" said his wife.

That night, Nicolas sneaked into their neighbor's garden and collected a handful of rapunzel; he then hurried home, shut the door behind him and said to his wife, "I've done it! I am never going back into that garden again!" The rapunzel really was bewitched, because after tasting the leaves, Anna refused to eat anything else. Nicolas decided to sneak back into the neighbor's garden. However, as he was returning home, his arms full of Rapunzel, he met the old witch.

"I . . . I am sorry! They are for my wife," Nicolas stammered. "She is expecting a baby and refuses to eat anything other than rapunzel. She is ill and I am very worried about her!"

The old woman pointed a skeletal finger at him and said: "She may have the rapunzel, but only on one condition!"

"Anything!" said Nicolas, desperate to get away.

"When your daughter is born, you must give her to me!" she said.

Nicolas was speechless! Give their long awaited baby to this woman in exchange for some rapunzel? It was ridiculous!

But Nicolas needed to get home. He would think of what to do later. "I . . . I promise you."

Satisfied, the old woman stepped aside and Nicolas fled.

On returning home he told Anna what had happened, but she just smiled. "The old woman was joking! She wanted to scare you and she certainly managed that!" Nicolas thought his wife must be right and they both forgot the incident.

Several months later a beautiful baby girl was born and she occupied their every thought.

After a few years, however, the old woman knocked on their door.

Nicolas and Anna tried to hide the little girl but the witch raised her stick and, whispering a spell, managed to take the girl from her mother's arms and vanished with her. Nobody knew where they had gone.

The witch named the child Rapunzel, and took her to a far-off land. Together they lived in a small house hidden deep in the forest. Only a few travelers ever visited those parts and the witch told everyone she was the child's grandmother, and the girl had been orphaned in a tragic accident. She said the same thing to little Rapunzel, who never doubted her words.

The witch became very fond of the girl. She showed her the kindness and the love of a real grandmother. She let her help mix potions and revealed to her the secrets for growing lush flowers and delicious vegetables. The only thing she did not allow her to do was stray too far from the house. She was very protective of the girl, and was so afraid of losing her that she forbade her to talk to anyone.

The years went by quickly and the child grew into a beautiful girl with long, golden hair. The witch decided to lock her inside a tower that was hidden by trees and completely surrounded by a thick, thorny hedge. Using a magic spell the witch made the stairs and the entrance to the tower disappear: the only opening that remained was a tiny window. Whenever the witch wanted to climb inside, she cried: "Rapunzel let down your hair, so that I may climb up to you." The poor girl spent the days alone and, unhappy about her sad fate, consoled herself by singing, which was her only joy.

One day a prince went by and, attracted by the girl's melodious voice, he approached the tower. When he saw the girl at the window, he immediately fell in love with her.

He searched for the door to the tower so he could reach her, but finally he had to give up as there was no door to be found. He soon realized that the poor young woman was imprisoned in the tower – no one could enter, nor could she escape.

Just then he heard footsteps and he quickly hid. From behind a tree, he saw an old woman making her way to the tower. Once there, she clapped her hands and shouted, "Rapunzel, Rapunzel, let down your hair!"

She had done this every day since she had been imprisoned in the tower. The witch grabbed hold of the hair, climbed up to the window and went into the tower.

A little while later, the prince saw the witch leave the same way that she had got in – using Rapunzel's long hair as a rope.

When he was sure that she had gone, he walked over to the tower and cried, "Rapunzel, Rapunzel, let down your hair."

At first she did not recognize the prince and she was very frightened and tried to hide, but when Rapunzel heard his gentle voice, and saw his kind eyes, she welcomed the prince. By now, Rapunzel had learned that the old woman was not really her grandmother but a witch who had taken Rapunzel from her parents when she was young. She told the prince that the witch didn't want Rapunzel to leave her, and so had kept her prisoner in the tower.

"I'll help you escape. I'll take you to the other side of the world, if need be, so she cannot find you," promised the prince. The two of them spent the rest of the night talking and at dawn, the prince slid down her long hair, stopping in the clearing to blow her a kiss. At that moment the witch came out of the forest and saw him.

Once the prince had gone, the witch walked over to the tower and called to Rapunzel as usual. She raised her stick, then softly whispered a spell. Immediately Rapunzel fell to the ground, asleep. Picking up a large pair of scissors, the witch cut off her long hair, and tied it tightly to the window.

She then cast a spell to make a long spiral staircase that led out of the tower. She hoisted the sleeping girl down the stairs and to a nearby cave.

The witch placed Rapunzel on the ground, and then found a large rock which she dragged across the entrance to the cave. At sunset the prince came to the tower as promised and called out to Rapunzel to help him climb up. The witch threw down Rapunzel's hair, and waited for him. The prince turned and came face to face with the witch.

"Where is she?" he said. "Where's Rapunzel?"

"She is imprisoned in a cave in the forest, where you will never find her." The witch raised her stick and began whispering a spell, and as the prince jumped back to avoid the spell, he fell through the window and into the spiny hedge below. He was battered and bruised, but he did not seem to be badly hurt. But when he opened his eyes, he discovered to his horror that the witch had managed to cast a spell on him after all – he was blind! He stumbled to his feet, and heard the witch scream, "You may still be alive, but you'll never find out where Rapunzel is!"

After several hours he heard the sound of sweet singing; he followed the music and came to a cave, the entrance of which was blocked by a large rock. He realized that this was where Rapunzel was and called to her. Working together, they managed to move the rock and Rapunzel threw herself into the prince's arms, finally free. When she saw what the witch had done to the prince, Rapunzel began to cry. Her tears fell on the prince's eyes, and broke the evil spell, so the prince was able to see again. However, the witch saw them from the tower; she picked up her stick and pointed at the bush below, casting a spell on it to turn it into a monster. In all her anger the witch accidentally fell on top of the bush and landed in the thorns, which grabbed hold of her and squeezed her until she suffocated. At last the lovers realized they were truly free.

One afternoon, Rapunzel was very quiet and thoughtful. "You look sad, my dear Rapunzel," said the prince. "What's wrong?"

"I was thinking about my parents. For years I thought they were dead, but I know the witch lied to me. I have been wondering where they are and dreaming of seeing them, but I know this is impossible."

"Maybe it isn't! I will send knights to every corner of the kingdom. They will visit every village, town or city. I am sure that we will find them."

But the weeks passed and there was no news. Finally, the day of the wedding came. Rapunzel felt so happy, but the day would not be perfect without her parents there. Suddenly the prince knocked on her door. "Rapunzel, I have a surprise!" he said.

"You cannot see the bride before the wedding. It's bad luck!" she said, laughing.

"In that case, I'll close my eyes, even if I will miss your smile."

Rapunzel opened the door and there were Nicolas and Anna, their eyes shining. She hugged them. Now her day was really perfect.

HANSEL AND GRETEL

At the edge of the woods lived a woodcutter who was so poor, he barely had enough food for his wife and his two small children, Hansel and Gretel. As time went by things gradually got worse, until he was no longer able to provide for them. One evening, when they were in the grip of hunger and despair the wife said to him: "Husband, we have no more food: tomorrow at dawn take the two children and give them each a small piece of bread, then take them into the woods with you, and when they are playing leave them there." Saddened and dismayed, the man exclaimed: "My wife, I don't have the courage to abandon my beloved children in the woods: the vicious beasts will surely kill them." His wife however was adamant: "If we keep going like this, we'll all starve to death," and she gave him no truce until the poor man gave in. That evening the two children, who were hungry and unable to sleep, heard what the mother said to the father. Gretel became frightened and began to weep, but Hansel said: "Sister, don't worry, I've got an idea." Without making any noise the boy stood up and slowly-slowly opened the door to go outside. The moon was shining brightly on the white pebbles on the ground. Hansel picked up a big handful of pebbles, hid them inside his pockets and returned home. "Sleep easy, Gretel," he said and promptly fell asleep himself.

At the break of dawn, the mother woke them both: "Get up children, today we go into the woods. Here is a small piece of bread for each of you, but don't be greedy, save it until lunch."

Gretel put all the bread in her apron because Hansel's pockets were full of pebbles, then they walked into the woods. Along the way, Hansel let the pebbles drop on the ground, one by one, without the parents noticing.

When they reached the depths of the woods, the father said: "Help gather some firewood to build a nice fire to keep us warm." Hansel and Gretel obeyed and when the fire was lit, the mother said: "Now lie next to the fire and rest; we are going to cut firewood. Wait here quietly, until we come back."

Hansel and Gretel remained beside the fire until noon, then they each ate a small piece of bread and trustingly waited until the evening for their parents to come back and get them.

By nightfall, Gretel became frightened but her brother said: "Don't despair, we just have to wait for the moon to rise." When the moon rose into the dark sky, Hansel took Gretel by the hand, the pebbles showing them the way home. They arrived home it was already morning . The father rejoiced to see his children safe and sound, whereas the mother only pretended to be happy. One evening Hansel and Gretel heard the mother say to the father: "Tomorrow you must lead the children into the deepest part of the woods so that they won't find their way back: there's no other way." The man followed his wife's demands. Hearing the mother's words, Hansel got up to go collect more pebbles, but this time the door was locked. He returned to his bed and said to Gretel: "Don't fret, the Lord will help us."

At daybreak the mother gave them a small piece of bread each. Along the path Hansel dropped the bread crumbs on the ground to mark the way. The mother had brought them to a part of the woods where they had never been before. The parents lit a fire and ordered the children to wait for them to return before nightfall. At nightfall, no one came for them. Hansel consoled Gretel and said: "Wait for the moon to rise, so we'll be able to see the bread crumbs I scattered to find the way home." When the moon rose Hansel looked for the bread crumbs but found none: the forest birds had eaten them all!

Overcome by anguish, Hansel and Gretel walked all night and all of the following day, until they fell asleep exhausted.

When they awoke, they continued walking and searching for the way home, but instead they ventured deeper into the woods. They became tired, discouraged and hungry and in the end, they drifted into a deep sleep.

On the third day, after having walked for many hours, they arrived at a strange little house made of candy and marzipan. The children were so hungry that in seeing all that goodness, they couldn't resist the temptation to dig in, but no sooner had Gretel started to gnaw at the door that a feeble voice came from inside: "Who's eating my candy house?"

The children did not answer and continued to eat. Suddenly the door opened and out came an old woman; Hansel and Gretel were so frightened that they dropped what they had in their hands.

Shaking her head, the old woman said: "How did you get here? Come on inside, you are welcome!" She took them by the hand and led them into the house where she cooked them a delicious dinner and prepared two beds with clean smelling sheets. Feeling safe, the children gratefully fell asleep.

In reality, the old woman was an evil witch who used her candy and marzipan house to attract children who were lost in the woods, and whenever she got her hands on one, she killed and cooked them, and ate them with great relish. That's why it's easy to understand why she was happy the two siblings had arrived at her house.

The following morning, before the kids woke up, the witch looked forward to a good feast and walked up to their beds to admire her prey.

Suddenly, before the poor boy could realize what was happening, she grabbed Hansel by the arm and locked him up inside a small cage.

Then she awoke Gretel with a jerk and said: "Go to the kitchen and prepare something good for your brother to eat, I want to fatten him up before I eat him!"

Gretel had no choice but to do as she was told.

Every day Hansel was forced to eat huge amounts of food while Gretel almost starved. Every day the witch approached the cage and said: "Hansel, let me feel your finger, I want to see if you are fat enough." But Hansel, who had understood she had poor eyesight, instead of his finger poked out a small chicken bone he kept hidden. So the old witch thought he hadn't gained any weight. One evening a few weeks later, the witch said to Gretel: "Fat of skinny, tomorrow I will kill your brother and cook him. In the meantime, I am going to make some bread to bake in the oven; go fetch me some water." Feeling desperate, Gretel fetched the water in which the following day Hansel was supposed to cook.

The next morning, the little girl lit the fire and hung the pot full of water from a hook. While Gretel was in the kitchen, shaking with sobs, the witch called her and said gruffly: "Go and lean into the oven and tell me if the bread is baked: I can't see all the way to the back." Her real plan was to shove Gretel into the oven, let her roast and then eat her in just a few bites. But Gretel, who had guessed the witch's intentions said: "I don't know how to look all the way to the back of the oven, show me first." And as soon as the witch leaned into the oven, Gretel gave her a big shove and quickly closed the door, securing it with an iron bolt. The witch began to scream, threatening her, then begging her, but Gretel ran off and left her to burn. She raced over to her brother and set him free.

The two children, embraced with great joy: at last, they could return to their parents!

The witch's house was filled with gold and gemstones: before setting off to find the way home, Hansel and Gretel took everything they could carry in their pockets and knapsacks. When they finally arrived, their father was overjoyed to see them again safe and sound. He'd been sad ever since abandoning his children, and the gold and gemstones that Hansel and Gretel brought home, allowed everyone to live without any more hardship.

CINDERELLA

A rich, recently widowed merchant took a difficult decision so as not to leave his young daughter alone during his long business journeys. Before setting off again he would re-marry so as to give the little girl a mother, even though he knew that no one could ever replace his wife in both their hearts.

His new wife already had two daughters and the widower hoped that the stepsisters would be pleasant playmates for his little girl, keeping her company and helping her bear her father's absence and the loss of her mother more easily.

So he set off on a long journey, without realizing that the stepmother would soon reveal herself to be a selfish, overbearing woman, and that the two stepsisters, vain and cruel like their mother, would make his little daughter's life very hard and sad. She was given the lowliest chores in the house: she had to do the dishes, clean the stairs and sweep her stepsisters' beautiful bedrooms; and when she had finished her work, there would be a biscuit, always covered in cinders, waiting for her near the fireplace. This was why her two sisters had given her the unkind nickname of Cinderella.

Long years passed in this way, without anything changing in Cinderella's life, but she never lost her sweet, kind nature. At last the moment came when things began to change: one day an invitation arrived for a great court ball, during which, it was said, the prince would choose his future wife.

Happy and excited, the two stepsisters spent days choosing the dresses and hairstyles that would suit them best, so that Cinderella had to iron heaps of linen and starch yards of brocade and lace.

At home all the talk was about the ball: "I," said the elder stepsister, "I shall wear the red velvet gown trimmed with English lace."

"And I," said the younger one, "shall wear my velvet gown with the mantle of gold flowers and a diamond necklace, so I shall be sure not go unnoticed."

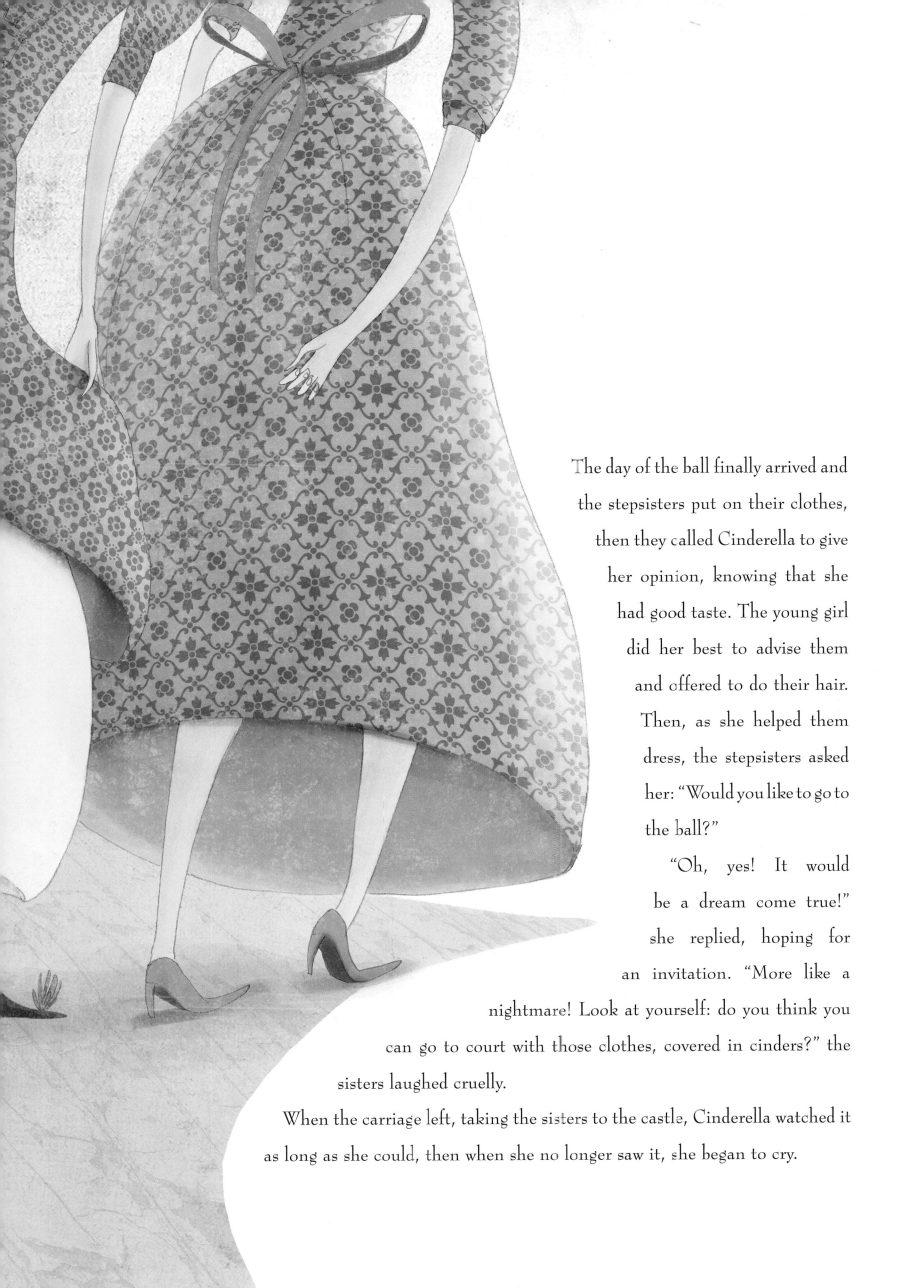

The day of the ball finally arrived and the stepsisters put on their clothes, then they called Cinderella to give her opinion, knowing that she had good taste. The young girl did her best to advise them and offered to do their hair. Then, as she helped them dress, the stepsisters asked her: "Would you like to go to the ball?"

"Oh, yes! It would be a dream come true!" she replied, hoping for an invitation. "More like a nightmare! Look at yourself: do you think you can go to court with those clothes, covered in cinders?" the sisters laughed cruelly.

When the carriage left, taking the sisters to the castle, Cinderella watched it as long as she could, then when she no longer saw it, she began to cry.

At that moment, a lady came up to her and asked what had happened. "Well, I would like…" but she was sobbing so hard that she was unable to speak. The lady, who was in fact a fairy, said to her: "I would like to see you happy tonight. So tell me: what would you like? To go to the ball?" "Yes, but I cannot: I am wearing rags and I do not know how to get to the castle, and also, what would I do if my stepmother recognized me?"

"No one will recognize you, little girl: foolish people usually judge by appearances, unfortunately, and your stepmother is no exception.

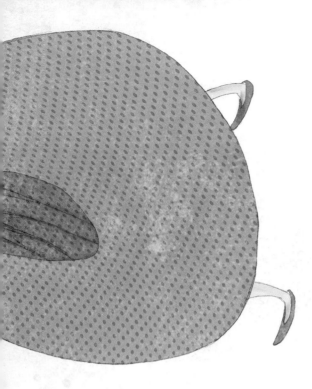

Looking at the lady you will become, she will only see a young noblewoman; she will not be able to see any similarity to the stepdaughter she left at home cleaning the house. Now I shall get to work. Fetch me a pumpkin."

"I shall go and get one from the vegetable garden," said Cinderella, confused. She did not see how a pumpkin could help her to go to the ball, but the lady was the first person to offer to help her for a long time and she did not want to stand in her way.

She took the largest pumpkin she could find in the garden and brought it to the fairy who, raising her hands, whispered a few words that Cinderella could not make out. At once the pumpkin began to grow and transform itself, until it had become an elegant carriage. At the sight of it Cinderella was speechless, but the fairy's magic had only just started!

A lizard sleeping on a branch became a liveried coachman and two little mice peeping out of their nest were transformed into white horses.

"It is done! So, Cinderella, are you ready?" asked the fairy, satisfied with her work. "I… yes, thank you so much, I cannot wait to go to the ball! But shall I wear these tattered old clothes?" Cinderella asked. "Oh, what a scatterbrain I am, my dear! No, absolutely not!" And in saying so, she gathered a handful of almond petals and threw them in the air.

As soon as she said the magic words, the almond petals turned into the most elegant gown the girl had ever seen. The fairy inspected her and with a critical look she said "Only the shoes are missing!" Then with a word she made two dainty shoes appear on Cinderella's feet: they were crystal and sparkled like diamonds. "Now you really look like a princess. But there is one condition: you must be home before the clock strikes midnight. Don't be late! And now go and have fun, my little one."

When Cinderella made her entrance, the whole ballroom fell silent: no one had ever seen a young girl so beautiful and with such a regal air. All the noblewomen in the ballroom immediately realized that they could never compete with her smile or her sparkling eyes.

Cinderella was the picture of happiness and the prince immediately realized that he wanted no one but her at his side that evening, so he approached and, with a bow, presented himself and asked her to dance. He then took her by the hand and danced all night with her: he did not want to dance with anyone else. Cinderella felt she was living a dream but when she heard the clock start striking midnight, she remembered the fairy's words and, whispering her excuses, she freed her hand from the prince's, rushed through the palace and ran down the stairs.

She lost one of her glass shoes but she did not stop, for fear that the prince would catch up with her.

Indeed, the prince had followed her down the staircase, determined to stop the mysterious young girl if only to discover her name, but he was only in time to see her climb into a sumptuous carriage and disappear into the night. Devastated, he suddenly saw the shoe that she had lost and picked it up with great care. When the two stepsisters returned from the ball, Cinderella asked them if they had had fun. Annoyed, the girls told her about the mysterious lady who had run away as midnight struck, who had been in such a rush that she had lost one of her glass shoes. The king's son had found it and picked it up and he had spent the rest of the ball gazing at it: naturally they were furious, assuming that he must have fallen madly in love with the beautiful girl who had lost her shoe.

And they were right, as they discovered a few days
later when the king's son asked the heralds to proclaim
that he would marry only the girl whose foot fitted this shoe.
He began by asking all the duchesses to try it on, then all the ladies
of the court, but with no success.

The two stepsisters were also asked to try on the shoe. Each did her best to force her
foot into it, but in vain. "Have you any other daughters, madam?" the page asked their
mother. "No!" she replied. "Then who is that young girl?" he asked, pointing at Cinderella
who was looking at her shoe in amazement from the top of the stairs. "She is only the
maid!" the exasperated stepmother replied. "I have orders to try the shoe on every young
girl in the kingdom," the royal servant said firmly. Cinderella approached and slipped
her foot into the shoe without any difficulty, ignoring the smirks of her sisters. The two
sisters were astonished and the stepmother suddenly recognized her as the beautiful lady
she had seen at the ball. Without a moment's hesitation they threw themselves at her feet
and asked her forgiveness for all the ill-treatment they had inflicted on her. Cinderella
told them to get up and embraced them, saying that she forgave them with all her heart;
then she followed the page to the carriage that would take her to the royal palace where she
could at last tell the prince her name and explain to him everything that had happened.

A month later a magnificent party took place during which Cinderella married the
prince and all the bells in the kingdom rang to celebrate the joyous event.

And from that day on the two young people lived happily ever after.

LITTLE RED RIDING HOOD

In a little cottage on the edge of the woods lived a little girl with her mother. She was loved by all for her cheerful, curious, sweet nature. The little girl, of course, had a name of her own, but because she always wore a red cloak with a hood, a present from her beloved grandmother, people had started calling her "Little Red Riding Hood," and the nickname pleased her so much that she adopted it. She was wearing her little red cloak when her mother gave her some bad news: "You grandmother will not be able to come to visit as she had promised you, my darling. Nothing serious has happened, but your grandmother has a bad cold so she has to stay in bed. She will not be able to get up for a few days: she has to rest!" "But how will she manage? Who will cook for her? Who will help her?" the little girl asked. "Let me go to her! I beg you, mama! I could stay with grandma for a few days and keep her company."

"I don't know: you'll have to go through the woods, you must be very careful…" said her mother anxiously. "I'll be careful! I promise!" said the girl.

"All right!" her mother said. "Take this basket with you, but please, follow the path!"

Little Red Riding Hood promised her mother that she would be careful, then she took the basket with a fruit tart and left. Immediately she forgot all her mother's advice! The forest was looking so lovely that day: the birds were singing and the squirrels were jumping from one tree to another: they amused the girl so much that she started following them.

In no time at all Little Red Riding Hood found herself in the middle of the forest, home to one of the most feared animals of the woods: the wolf.

The wolf could hear Little Red Riding Hood laughing from afar and decided to investigate.

He made his way through the bushes, saying to himself: "A little girl in the middle of the forest? Bad for her and good for me: I am about to have a delicious little meal!" And as he said this, he came out of his hiding place, walked towards her and asked her with a sinister smile: "Hello, little girl, what is your name? And what are you doing in this part of the forest?"

"I am Little Red Riding Hood, I am going to visit my grandmother who is ill." On hearing her reply, the wolf began toying with the idea of gobbling up both Little Red Riding Hood and the grandmother, but to do this he would have to get to the grandmother's house before Little Red Riding Hood! There he would attack the grandmother and then wait for the granddaughter to arrive. But first he had to get rid of the girl for long enough to reach the grandmother's house. The wolf flashed his long, sharp teeth beneath his whiskers, then asked the girl: "Wouldn't you like to take her flowers too?"

"I love flowers! They would be perfect to cheer up my grandmother," Little Red Riding Hood replied excitedly, "Wolf, please tell me where I can find them."

"Continue along that path until you get to a waterfall," the wolf explained, telling the girl a much longer way along the main road so as to give himself enough time to reach the grandmother's house before her. Little Red Riding Hood set off in the direction indicated by the animal.

"Good girl, go into the forest while I run to your grandmother's house!" the wolf thought to himself, watching the girl until she disappeared behind a big oak tree.

When he was sure that Little Red Riding Hood would not be turning back, the wolf made his way in the opposite direction and ran to the grandmother's house, arriving there well before Little Red Riding Hood! The wolf laughed: had made it in time for his plan to succeed.

He knocked at the door, cleared his throat and then, imitating the little girl's voice, he said: "It's me, grandma, Little Red Riding Hood."

"Little one, you have come to visit me? Come in, my dear, the door is open."

And the wolf went in, leapt on the bed and gobbled up the grandmother in a single mouthful. Then he lay down in the grandmother's bed, having put on her clothes, her bonnet and her glasses.

As he had expected, Little Red Riding Hood soon arrived. When she knocked on the door, the wolf imitated the grandmother's voice, asking: "Who is it?"

"It's me, Little Red Riding Hood," the girl replied. "What a lovely surprise, my dear, do come in and say hello to your grandmother!" The little girl pushed the door open, walked to the bed and said: "Grandma, you look strange to me! What big eyes you have!"

"All the better to see you with, my dear," the wolf replied.

"And what big ears you have!"

"All the better to hear you with."

"And what a big mouth you have!"

"All the better to eat you with!" the wolf shouted, leaping on the little girl. And in no time at all no trace remained of Little Red Riding Hood.

Some say that this was the end of the story: the wolf, feeling full, left the cottage and walked contentedly into the thick of the forest. But others say that, while the wolf was snoring in the grandmother's bed, a hunter passing by the cottage heard the noise and went in.

He saw the wolf fast asleep with his belly bloated. So he took out his knife and was about to attack when the animal's belly suddenly moved. He cut open the wolf's stomach and, to his surprise, Little Red Riding Hood and her grandmother jumped out, terrified and in a sorry state but safe and sound! They embraced each other, then thanked the hunter sincerely: "I had given up all hope of anyone being able to save us!" the grandmother said, deeply moved. "I had been trying to catch this wolf for a long time," the hunter replied. "Today is a very special day for me. Now I can go home." In saying so, the hunter hoisted the heavy corpse of the wolf onto his shoulders and walked slowly home, leaving Little Red Riding Hood and her grandmother to celebrate with a slice of fruit tart and plenty of cuddles.

LITTLE BRIAR ROSE

Once upon a time there were a king and queen, rulers of a country far away, over which they reigned with kindness and generosity.

They had been married for many years, but they had no children and although they had long hoped one day to have a child, the couple's wish had never come true.

At last one day their dream was fulfilled and the queen gave birth to a baby girl, who was named Rosamond, like the goddess of the dawn, because they soon discovered that the little creature could fill their lives with light. Even the court seemed to be lit up by the child's smile and, a little later, frantic preparations were being made for the solemn ceremony that was to be held in the castle in honor of the little girl.

Every corner of the building was swept and polished by the servants, who prepared a hundred guest rooms. A week before the ceremony the cooks began kneading, chopping and roasting, and the waiters polished the gold tableware reserved for the most important guests.

Hundreds of invitations were written by hand in gold ink and the fastest riders delivered them to the four corners of the kingdom, but it was the king himself who wrote the invitations for those who were closest to his heart, for the fairies who lived in the kingdom, so that they could be godmothers to the child.

The king invited seven fairies, but originally there were eight sisters of the magical woods. There was also the old fairy of the mountain, who no one remembered any more, because for decades she had lived alone in her cave, devoting herself to the study of the black arts. Eventually the day of the long-awaited ceremony arrived, as did the guests who began entering the castle from the first light of dawn.

During the party, the guests came up to the cradle to show the baby the gifts that they had brought.

Finally the fairy godmothers approached and gave Rosamond the most precious things imaginable, endowing her with the greatest virtues through their spells. But when the last fairy came to offer the child her gift of happiness, a gust of wind threw open the doors of the castle and dense black smoke invaded the hall, at the center of which the eighth fairy appeared: the old mountain witch, who was angry and offended by the fact that she had not been invited.

"What's going on? Who are you?" asked the king, rushing to hold Rosamond, who had burst into tears at the sight of the old woman.

"This is the girl you did not want me to know?" said the old woman.

"This is our daughter," said the king, "Who are you?"

"I am a much more powerful sorceress than these fairies will ever be and I cannot stand being ignored: it is an unacceptable insult."

"I am sorry that you have taken offense," said the king, "I pray you, please sit down next to us. I hope you can forgive us."

"Of course, Your Majesty, but only if I myself can give the little princess a gift," said the sorceress with a mischievous smile.

Then she lifted her wand, pointed it at the girl and said, "When the princess turns eighteen she will prick her finger with a needle and die." Having said this, the cruel fairy wrapped herself in a black cloud and disappeared as quickly as she had come, leaving the king and queen desperate and the whole court terrified.

When the smoke had cleared, the youngest fairy, who had been interrupted by the arrival of the witch, said shyly: "I may have the solution."

"My powers are not enough to lift the curse laid on the baby, but I have not yet given my gift to the princess and I can use it to lighten the terrible revenge of the witch," she explained.

Then she added: "If she is pricked with a needle, Rosamond will not die, but she will fall asleep for a hundred years, together with the whole court, and only the kiss of true love will awaken her." The king and queen were relieved, but they also made a decision: for the safety of the princess, from that day on no one in the kingdom was allowed to keep needles and spindles in the house. "This will surely protect our daughter," said the king, embracing the queen and the baby. Years passed without anything unusual happening. As the fairies had predicted, the princess grew up and became a kind, cheerful girl, happy and inquisitive. Unfortunately it was exactly this last characteristic that got her into trouble, just as the court was preparing a big party to celebrate her eighteenth birthday. Waiting for the party to begin, Rosamond was bored and she began to wander around the castle.

She reached a tall tower, at the top of which she found a room that she had never entered. "How strange, I didn't know there was a room up here!" said the princess as she opened the door.

The first thing she saw was an old woman who was spinning with a spindle. "Come in my dear, I am glad to have some company," said the old woman, inviting her to come closer. "What are you doing here, what is this?" the young girl asked. "It is a spindle, princess. It is used for spinning. Would you like to try it?"

Rosamond had never seen this device and she picked it up, but in doing so she pricked her finger and a little drop of blood emerged. Immediately the princess felt weak and tired.

The last thing she heard was the laughter of the old woman, who had turned into the mountain witch and was now rejoicing at having accomplished her revenge, while Rosamond and the entire court fell into a magic, deep sleep. Gradually the castle was surrounded by an impenetrable forest of thorns that encircled and completely covered it, so much so that the flags flying on the roof were no longer visible.

Over the years the legend spread throughout the country: the legend of the sleeping princess, waiting in the highest tower of the castle to be saved by a kiss of love, but none of the suitors could ever penetrate the forest of brambles.

Finally a young prince arrived in the kingdom eager to take on the challenge, not knowing that on that very day the period of one hundred years established by the spell would be over. When he approached the mass of thorns, he found beautiful flowers that spontaneously moved aside so that he could easily enter the castle.

Looking for the princess, he crossed the large halls where he saw the noblemen and their servants lying down, sleeping next to each other. High up on the throne, the king and queen slept embracing each other.

The prince passed them by and went up to the little room in which Rosamond was sleeping with a sweet smile on her face.

Deeply moved, he entered and approached the princess, looking at her serene, beautiful face for a long time, then he came closer to touch her lips with a kiss. In that instant, the room lit up as if the sun of a new dawn was rising. When the rays of light touched the face of the princess, she suddenly blinked and slowly opened her eyes. So Rosamond awoke from her deep sleep and, with her, the whole court. From that day, for over a month, festivities took place in the palace to celebrate the awakening of the court and the marriage of Rosamond, who was blessed by the spells of her sweet fairy godmothers.

SNOW WHITE

During a cold winter morning, the queen sat by the window. For some time, she and her husband, the king, desired to become parents; how wonderful their life would be with a child! While lost in thought, she accidentally pricked her finger and a drop of blood trickled out. As she watched this, she thought, "I wish for a charming and cheerful child, with lips as red as this drop of blood, hair as black as coal, and skin as white as snow." A good fairy must have heard the queen's prayer, because soon after, her wish came true. When the child was born, she was named Snow White. But soon, the queen was struck by an unknown illness, which none of the doctors summoned from all over the kingdom were able to cure.

For months after the queen's death, the king spent all his time comforting his daughter.

But as he had many duties, the kingdom needed him to rule. He decided to marry again. When the new bride's carriage arrived at court one cold autumn morning, the crowd that gathered to see her was enchanted. She curtsied before the king, who greeted her, then entered the castle followed by two footmen who carefully carried a large, heavy parcel shrouded in cloth. When she was alone in her room, the queen approached the parcel and, throwing the cloth aside, revealed a mirror that she propped up against the wall. No one suspected that in reality, she was a powerful witch. The mirror, which she took with her everywhere, was magic. Looking at it she said, "Mirror, mirror on the wall, who is the fairest of them all?"

At that, the mirror came alive. From inside golden sparks arose, which began to swirl and finally took the shape of a face that replied, "My queen, in all the kingdom, there is none more beautiful than you."

Every evening, the queen looked in the mirror, and every time she asked the same question and heard the same answer.

As the years passed, Snow White grew up looking more and more like her mother from whom she had inherited kindness, gaiety and beauty.

One day, when hearing Snow White's laughter, the stepmother went out on the balcony, suddenly she noticed that Snow White had become a beautiful young woman.

"Surely, no woman in the world is more beautiful than me!" The queen hurried back to her chambers and, as she uncovered the mirror, she thought there was only one way to be sure.

"Mirror, mirror on the wall, who is the fairest of them all?" she asked.

"You will not be happy with what I have to say. Your Majesty, you are beautiful, but Snow White is more beautiful than you," the mirror replied.

When she heard these words, the queen became furious. The next day, she summoned the royal huntsman.

When the man arrived she said, "Huntsman, I have a special task for you that must remain between us."

"My queen, I will do anything you ask!" he said.

"You must kill Snow White!" whispered the queen.

"Take her into the woods, today. When you return, say there was a tragic accident and she died. Bring me her heart in this!" She gave the huntsman's a bejeweled box.

Snow White loved the woods and was glad the huntsman suggested a walk. The huntsman, however, held his head low. He knew if he didn't kill Snow White, the queen would not spare his life. When Snow White's back was turned, he pulled out his knife and slowly approached her intending to kill her. Yet, at the last moment, he cried, "I can't! My child, I cannot harm you!"

Snow White saw the knife in the huntsman's hand and the tears streaming down his cheeks. The man fell to his knees and confessed everything.

"My stepmother? I... I don't believe it!" Snow White exclaimed.

"You must, my child. This woman is evil and will stop at nothing to destroy you!" he huntsman said. "But where shall I go?" Snow White was weeping.

"It doesn't matter child! Go now! Run! RUN!" the huntsman cried.

Snow White embraced him then fled.

The huntsman watched her and then he walked further into the woods. He found a wild boar and killed it with his bow. He put its heart into the bejeweled box, then returned to the castle where the queen waited impatiently. "Well?" she asked when he arrived at her quarters. "Have you done what I ordered?"

"Yes, Your Majesty. You no longer need to worry about Snow White," he said, giving her the box. When she opened it, she began to laugh uncontrollably.

Meanwhile Snow White was terrified. She had never been in the woods at night.

In the darkness, the trees that she climbed during the day seemed scary, their branches looked like monstrous arms wanting to grab her.

She ran for hours, without knowing where she was going. At last, she caught sight of a cottage at the center of a clearing. Through a window, she saw the glowing light of an open fire. Snow White stood at the door and knocked timidly. There was no reply. Snow White knocked harder and the door opened slightly. There was no one home.

"I could wait by the fire until the owner comes back."

Snow White looked around and was surprised that everything in the room was pint-sized. The table was set with seven little plates, and on the dresser she saw that there were such tiny cups. By the fire there was a chair like the one she had as a child. In the corner of the room there was a staircase, which she decided to climb. She found seven tiny beds. She was so tired that she lay down on one and fell fast asleep. Soon after, the cottage's inhabitants returned. They were seven dwarfs who certainly didn't expect to find a beautiful girl fast asleep in one of their beds.

"She is beautiful!" whispered the youngest. "Shh! Don't shout! You'll wake her!" said the wisest.

"I am already awake," said Snow White, opening her eyes.

"I'm Snow White and I am sorry to have come into your house without permission, but I didn't know where else to go. I no longer have a home," said Snow White, her eyes bright with tears.

"In that case you must stay!" the youngest dwarf said.

Meanwhile, the stepmother was in her room standing before the mirror. When she asked who the most beautiful woman was, the mirror replied, "You are the most beautiful within the castle

walls, but Snow White is still alive, and she is more beautiful than you."

"What? But that's impossible!" cried the queen. "Prove that she is still alive!"

Snow White's face appeared in the mirror. She was laughing, surrounded by the seven dwarfs. In seeing this, the queen became pale. "The huntsman lied to me," she hissed. "I will have to go to Snow White myself."

In a flash, the queen left the room and ran down the castle stairs into the cellar where she kept books on black magic hidden.

She grabbed a huge pot underneath which she lit a greenish fire. One by one, she added the ingredients to the cauldron, concocting a ghastly mixture. When it was ready, she dipped an apple into the fuming brew. She then prepared a magic potion that she drank to transform herself into a grinning old fruit seller.

And so she set out into the woods. Meanwhile, in the cottage, Snow White was unaware of having been discovered by the stepmother and, without suspecting her evil plans, she was enjoying herself: dancing, singing and playing music with her new friends!

The next morning, while the dwarfs were at work mining for gemstones, Snow White cleaned the house, washed the laundry, then decided to bake a lovely cake.

At that same moment, she heard a voice calling, "Apples! Red, juicy apples!"

It was an old woman, carrying a basket filled with the most beautiful apples Snow White had ever seen.

"Just in time!"

"It's your lucky day, my dear. These apples will make a delicious pie," the queen said. "Here, try one."

She offered Snow White the reddest and shiniest apple in the basket, and as soon as Snow White bit into it, her head began to swim. She then fell to the floor and everything went black. When the dwarfs returned home, they found Snow White lying on the ground next to the bitten apple. After trying desperately to revive her, they realized there was nothing they could do to awaken the girl from a sleep that seemed as deep as death itself. The seven dwarfs decided they would lay their friend in an open crystal coffin in the middle of the clearing. They spent days carving the rock. When it was ready, they placed Snow White inside and decorated it with flowers.

The summer passed and fall arrived, but Snow White did not awaken. After many months of grief, the dwarfs knew she never would.

One day, when they came home from work, they saw a young nobleman standing beside the crystal coffin. He was riding past the clearing when he saw Snow White lying there.

"Stop! Don't you dare touch her!" the dwarfs shouted, clutching their pickaxes in their hands. "I mean her no harm," said the young man, not taking his eyes off her captivating face. "Is she sleeping?" he asked.

"She is the victim of a spell," they explained. "There is no way to wake her up."

The prince, who had fallen madly in love with the girl, begged the dwarfs to let him bring Snow White to his castle, where he would watch over her with the utmost dedication. The dwarfs agreed, albeit reluctantly, so the prince called his servants to load the case into a carriage. The crystal bed was heavy and one of the servants, stumbling on a root, jolted it harshly. It actually had a miraculous effect: the movement caused the piece of apple preventing Snow White from breathing to fall out of her mouth, bringing her back to life.

Suddenly her beautiful face became animated: she blinked and turned to look at the young man, smiling. The prince took her hand and asked her to follow him to his castle to marry him. Snow White agreed happily. She said goodbye to the dwarfs, hugging them one by one, and climbed up onto the prince's horse, riding away with him to a future of long years of happiness.

THE SIX SWANS

While out on a hunt one day, a king chased his prey into a forest so thick that he lost his way home. While he was trying in vain to find his way out of the trees, he saw an old lady approaching who was bent over under the weight of her years and who was, in reality, a witch. The king politely asked her to show him the right way and the old woman answered him hoarsely: "Certainly Your Majesty, but there is one condition – that you marry my daughter and make her a queen. You should know that without my help, you will never manage to get out of the forest and you will end up dying of hardship." Frightened by her words, the king let himself be guided out of the woods by his future bride. The sovereign was a widower and had seven children, six boys and a girl, who he loved more than anything else in the world. Fearing that their new stepmother might do them harm, he decided to take them far away to an isolated castle in the middle of a forest. The castle could only be accessed using a path that was so difficult to find that the king himself would not have succeeded if a sorceress had not given him a ball of wool that, when thrown to the ground, rolled by itself, indicating the path. The king often went to visit his children and his long absences ended up making the queen suspicious. She discovered her husband's secret from a servant and took possession of the magic ball of wool. Then she sewed seven small little shirts and set off for the castle. When she arrived, the children ran towards her, unaware of the imminent danger. In a quick move, the stepmother threw the shirts she had sewn onto the six little princes, who immediately turned into swans and flew away. Convinced that she had finally freed herself of all her stepchildren, she returned home satisfied, unaware of the existence of the little girl, who had not run out to meet her.

The next day, when the king came to the castle, he found only the little girl, who told him what had happened and showed him the feathers that her brothers, transformed into swans, had dropped into the courtyard. Unable to believe that the queen had cast such a spell, the king decided to take the little girl with him but she begged him to let her spend one last night in the castle. When it was dark, the girl fled into the woods. She walked all night and all the next day and was at the end of her strength when she finally saw a cabin. She entered shyly, but saw no one, so went upstairs, where she found a room with six beds. Tired and afraid, she decided to lie down under the beds to rest for a little while. When the sun went down, she heard a flutter of wings and saw six swans coming in through the window. Slowly they settled on the ground and began to blow on each other until all their feathers fell off; then they removed the swan skin like a shirt. To her great astonishment, the girl saw her brothers again: full of joy, she jumped out of her hiding place and ran to embrace them. Unfortunately, their joy soon turned into worry. The cabin was actually the hideout of a group of dangerous, bloodthirsty robbers and the six princes would not be able to protect their little sister because they could resume human form for only fifteen minutes each night, before turning once again into swans.

After listening to their words, the young girl asked her brothers: "Is there no way I can free you from this cruel spell?"

Sadly the brothers replied: "It would be too difficult: for six years, you would have to not speak or laugh and in the meantime, you would have to sew us six shirts made of aster flowers. If you speak even a single word, it would all be in vain."

They just barely finished these words before they again turned into six beautiful swans, ready to fly away.

But the little girl would not give up and decided that she would free her brothers even at the cost of her own life.

The next morning she went to collect asters then she climbed up a tall tree and began to sew. She would not speak, nor laugh, nor do anything except sew. A long time had already passed by, when one day the king of the country went hunting in the woods. His squires saw the girl in the tree and ordered her to come down. The princess, unable to answer, merely shook her head, so the men, irritated, went to get her and took her to their king, who asked her who she was in all the languages he knew, without receiving any answer. The princess was beautiful and the king, despite her silence, fell madly in love with her, so he took her to the castle, where he married her a few days later in a lavish ceremony. Their marriage did not sit well with the queen mother, who was secretly evil, so she tried in every way to show her daughter-in-law in a bad light, even accusing her of witchcraft. But the queen continued to sew her shirts without thinking about anything else. She was eventually accused of having practiced black magic on her three children, who the queen mother had actually stolen and concealed from her. The king was left with no choice but to hand her over to the court that condemned her to die at the stake. The day of her execution coincided with the end of the six years of silence for the young woman, who in the meantime had almost completed the shirts for her brothers: there was only one sleeve left to complete. When they led her to the stake, she took the shirts with her and held them close to her heart. Just as the fire was about to be lit, she looked up at the sky with a last gesture of hope and saw six majestic swans flying by. With a fluttering of wings, they landed beside her and she threw their shirts on them: in an instant, their swan skins fell off and the six princes appeared, finally freed from their stepmother's spell. The youngest brother, in place of his left arm, was left with a swan wing. The siblings hugged, finally together, and then the queen went to the king who had astonishingly witnessed the whole scene. "My beloved spouse," she said to him, "I am finally allowed to speak and I can prove that I have been unjustly accused." She told him how the queen mother had slandered her, how she had taken her children away, hiding them so that everyone would believe that she had killed them cruelly. The king ordered a search for the princes to be brought home and that the evil mother-in-law was to be burned at the stake as a witch. The bad times had passed and the king, the queen and her six brothers lived happily ever after.

MANUELA ADREANI was born in Rome and later moved to Turin where she currently lives. After completing a diploma in illustration, she worked as a graphic designer before moving into the world of animation. She won a scholarship for a masters in animation at IED Turin then worked for the "Lastrego e Testa" studio on the television series *The Adventures of Aladdin* and *Amita in the Jungle*, produced and broadcast by RAI, and on the short film "Creation", made for the eponymous book by Carlo Fruttero.

In 2011, she ventured into freelance illustration, working with Benchmark and Scholastic India.

Manuela was among the winners of the illustration competition held to commemorate the 130th anniversary of the publication of Pinocchio. More recently she has illustrated several titles for White Star Kids.

Text adaptation
VALERIA MANFERTO DE FABIANIS

Graphic Layout
PAOLA PIACCO

WSkids
WHITE STAR KIDS

© 2019 White Star s.r.l.
Piazzale Luigi Cadorna, 6 - 20123 Milan, Italy
www.whitestar.it

Translation: Aubrey Lawrence and Contextus s.r.l., Pavia, Italy
and TperTradurre s.r.l.

ISBN 978-88-544-1355-9
1 2 3 4 5 6   23 22 21 20 19

Printed in Poland